W9-CLD-375

GROWN-UPS GET TO DO ALL THE DRIVING

By William Steig

MICHAEL DI CAPUA BOOKS
HARPERCOLLINS PUBLISHERS

FRANKLIN PIERCE
COLLEGE LIBRARY
RINDGE, N.H. 03461

Copyright © 1995 by William Steig

All rights reserved

Library of Congress catalog card number: 94-76833

Printed in the United States of America

Designed by Susan Mitchell

First edition, 1995

CURR
PZ
7
.S8177
Gr
1995

For Holly McGhee

GROWN-UPS WANT CHILDREN TO BE HAPPY

GROWN-UPS LIKE TO PUNISH PEOPLE

GROWN-UPS MAKE YOU GO TO THE DENTIST

GROWN-UPS LIKE HANDS TO BE CLEAN

GROWN-UPS ALWAYS WANT TO BE KISSED

GROWN-UPS ARE ALWAYS WEIGHING THEMSELVES

GROWN-UPS ALWAYS HAVE TO KNOW WHAT TIME IT IS

GROWN-UPS MEASURE EVERYTHING

GROWN-UPS DO LOTS OF EXERCISE

GROWN-UPS CAN'T RUN

GROWN-UPS GET TIRED EASILY

GROWN-UPS TAKE LIBERTIES

GROWN-UPS LOVE RESTAURANTS

GROWN-UPS LIKE PARTIES

GROWN-UPS LIKE TO SLEEP LATE

GROWN-UPS LIKE TO WATCH OTHER PEOPLE PLAY

GROWN-UPS ARE ALWAYS HAVING "DISCUSSIONS"

GROWN-UPS HOG THE TELEPHONE

GROWN-UPS WANT TO KNOW

WHAT'S GOING ON IN THE WHOLE WORLD

GROWN-UPS HATE TO ANSWER QUESTIONS

GROWN-UPS LIKE CHILDREN TO BE POLITE

GROWN-UPS CAN BE SO RUDE

GROWN-UPS GET BALD

GROWN-UPS CAN TAKE OUT THEIR TEETH

GROWN-UPS SNORE

GROWN-UPS GET HEADACHES

GROWN-UPS GET WRINKLES

GROWN-UPS HIDE THINGS

GROWN-UPS HATE TO PAY THEIR TAXES

GROWN-UPS TAKE A LOT OF PILLS

GROWN-UPS GET TO DO ALL THE DRIVING

FRANKLIN PIERCE COLLEGE LIBRARY

00104230

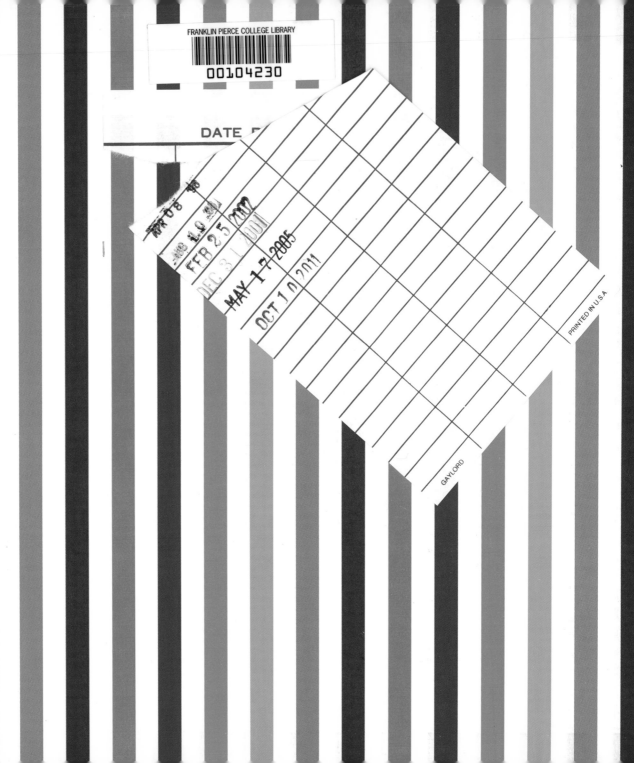

DATE